Trouble with a Puddle

www.dk.com
LONDON • NEW YORK • STUTTGART • SYDNEY

www.dk.com

Editor Vicci Parr
Designers Mandy Sherliker and Ness Wood
Managing Editor Joanna Devereux
Managing Art Editor Chris Fraser
Production Linda Dare
DTP Designer Jill Bunyan
Original TV Script Sally-Ann Lever
Story Adaptation Caryn Jenner
Photography Dave King
Illustrations Denis Ryan

First published in Great Britain in 1999 by
Dorling Kindersley Limited, 9 Henrietta Street, London WC2E 8PS

A CIP record for this book is available from the British Library.

ISBN 0-7513-6650-1

Colour reproduction by Dot Gradations Limited
Printed in Belgium by Proost

It was time for Mopatop to open his shop.
"Welcome to Mopatop's Shop," he said.
"Would you like perfume that's smelly?
Or a creature called
Yelley? Or a
flower named
Shelley?"

In the attic, it was Moosey's bath time.
"Do you want some help, Moosey?" his mother called from the kitchen.
"No thanks, Mum," Moosey called back.

He poured some bubble bath into the water. Mmmm. That smelled good. Moosey poured the rest of the bubble bath in and got ready for his bath.

In the shop, Shelley was thirsty.
"Any chance of a drink, Mopatop?"
she asked from the little doorway.
"Of course, Shelley. Right away."
Mopatop sprinkled Shelley
with cold water.

DRIP.
"What was that noise?" wondered Mopatop.
"It sounded like a drip. Did it come from over there?"
DRIP.
"Or up there?"

DRIP.
Mopatop looked here and there but he couldn't find the drip anywhere.
DING!
"That bell means I've got a customer," he said.

Mopatop's customer was a squid.
"Hello, Ozzie," Mopatop greeted him.
"How are your new wellington boots?"
"They're lovely," said
Ozzie. "I've just got
a little problem.

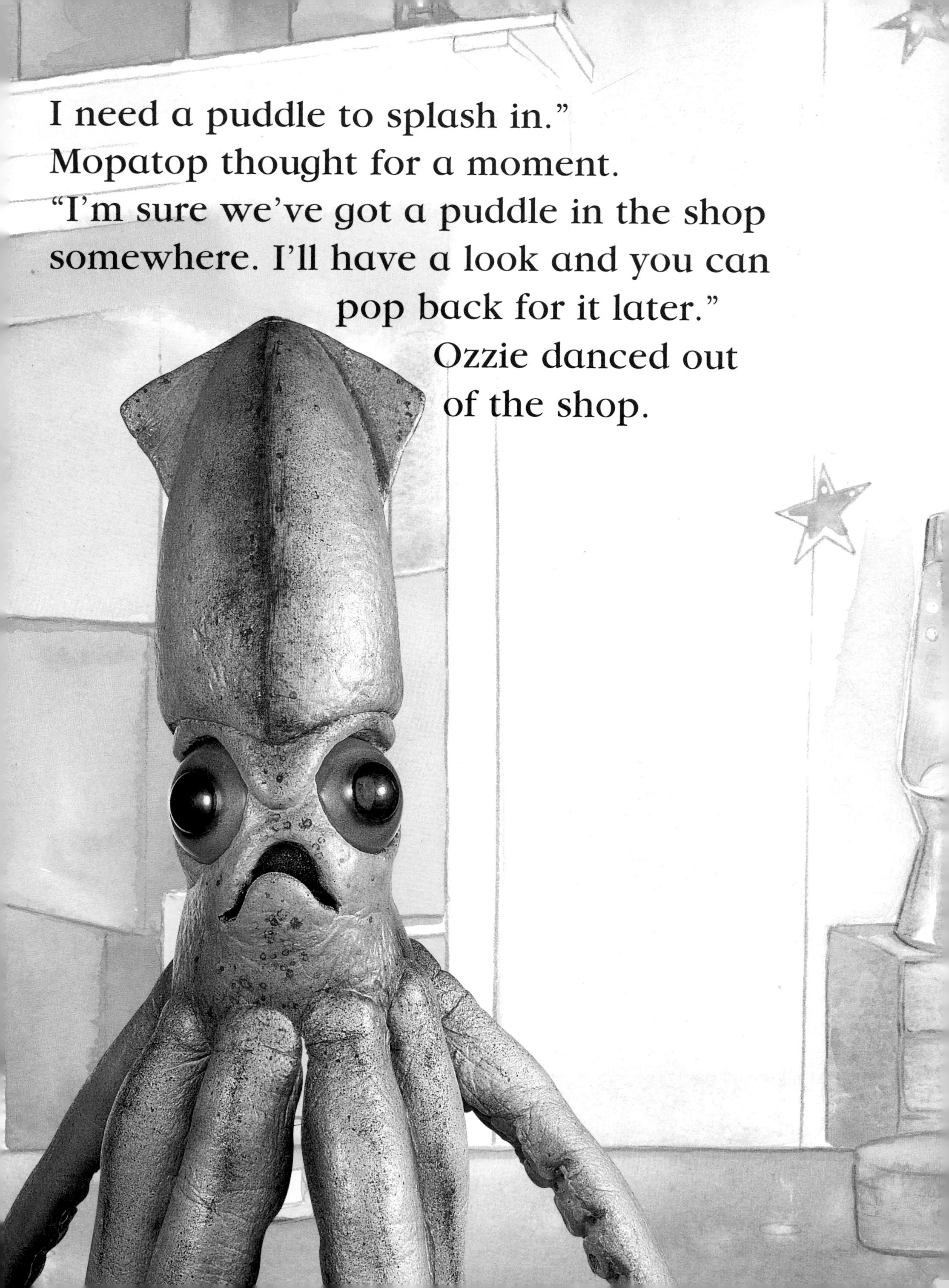

I need a puddle to splash in."
Mopatop thought for a moment.
"I'm sure we've got a puddle in the shop somewhere. I'll have a look and you can pop back for it later."
Ozzie danced out of the shop.

"Hello, Mopatop," said
Puppyduck. "What's
the matter?"
"Ozzie wants a puddle,
but I'm all in a muddle,"
Mopatop replied. "Where can. . ."
DRIP. DRIP.
Puppyduck looked up at the
water dripping from the ceiling.

Mopatop was still thinking about Ozzie.
"Puppyduck, where can we look
for Ozzie's puddle?"
"Let's look in the Rainy
Day Box," suggested
Puppyduck.

In the Rainy Day Box, they found pencils, paper and stickers. But there was no puddle. "Oh dear," said Mopatop. "This is the box for things to do *inside* on a rainy day. We need the box for things to do *outside* on a rainy day, like puddles for splashing."

DRIP. DRIP. DRIP.
"Mopatop, look over there!" said Puppyduck, pointing towards the corner of the shop. Mopatop turned to see drops of water dripping from the ceiling.
"There's a leak in the shop!" said Mopatop.

In the attic, Moosey was enjoying his bath.
He began to sing:

Splashing around, don't you love it?
Splashing around, yes I love it!

"Moosey, don't splash!"
called his mother.
"You'll flood Mopatop's shop."
"Don't worry, Mum," Moosey called back,
accidentally splashing more bubbles onto
the floor.

In the shop, Mopatop and Puppyduck found some buckets to catch the drips. They found some umbrellas, too.

"We've got to stop this leak," sighed Mopatop. "But we still haven't found a puddle for Ozzie!"
DING!
"Here he comes now," said Puppyduck.

"Hello, hello!" said Ozzie. "I'm so excited! May I have my puddle now, please?"

Mopatop and Puppyduck looked at each other anxiously.

"Ozzie, I'm sorry," said Mopatop. "We haven't been able to find your puddle."

"I see," said Ozzie, disappointed.

"More drips!" cried Puppyduck.
Mopatop gave Ozzie an umbrella and rushed over to help Puppyduck.
"I'll be with you in a minute, Ozzie," he called.

Ozzie sighed. He looked up at the drops dripping from the ceiling. Then he looked down at the floor. . .

. . .and saw a puddle!
“Look at that!” said Ozzie. “It’s wonderful!”
He put on his boots and jumped into
the puddle.
SPLASH! SPLASH! SPLASH!
Ozzie began to sing:

Splashing around,
don’t you
love it?

In the attic, Moosey was singing too:

Splashing around, yes I love it!

Moosey had splashed his bath
water all over the floor.
"Bath time is such fun!" he laughed.

In the shop, Mopatop and Puppyduck watched Ozzie splashing in his puddle.

"I love it!" Ozzie exclaimed. "It's a perfect puddle!"
Mopatop liked a happy customer.
"I told you we had a puddle somewhere, Ozzie."
Ozzie took off his boots and smiled.

Moosey stepped out of the bath.
"Are you sure you don't need any help?" his mother called.

Moosey looked at the wet floor.
"I could use some help tidying up, Mum."

Downstairs in the shop,
the drips had stopped dripping
and the big clock chimed.
"It's time to close the shop,"
said Mopatop.
Puppyduck wrapped Ozzie's
puddle in a bag and
waved goodbye.

"Well, Puppyduck, we'd better tidy the shop," said Mopatop. "Where's the mop?" Mopatop and Puppyduck began to clean up the shop.